THE EXTRAORDINARY INVENTION

THE EXTRAORDINARY INVENTION

Bernice Myers

Macmillan Publishing Company
New York
Collier Macmillan Publishers
London

Macmillan Publishing Company
866 Third Avenue, New York, N.Y. 10022
Collier Macmillan Canada, Inc.
Printed in the United States of America
10 9 8 7 6 5 4 3 2 1

Library of Congress Cataloging in Publication Data

Myers, Bernice.
The extraordinary invention.

Summary: Sally and her father, who love to invent
things together, make a time machine as a present
for Sally's mother—only something goes terribly
wrong.
[1. Inventions—Fiction]   I. Title.
PZ7.M9817Ex 1984   [E]   84-3884
ISBN 0-02-767780-X

To Effie
A golden head
Tall and upright
A splendid flower.

Sally
and her father
are inventors.
They build their
inventions
out of scraps
and old parts
they find in
junkyards.

Their house is
filled
with extraordinary
machines...

...like the Sneaker Finder

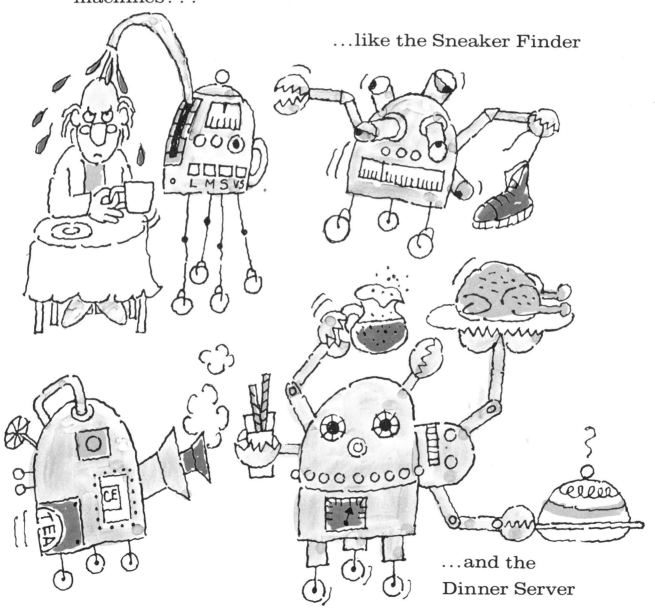

...and the
Dinner Server

...and the
Clothes Picker Upper

...and the Door Closer.

One day
Sally said
to her father,
"Let's surprise Mama
and invent something
just for her."

"Yes! Yes!
Just for her!
Something special!
Good idea!
I know just what
will please her."

And they began
at once
to build their machine.
They worked very hard...
sometimes forgetting
to eat or sleep.

"Hugo!
Come to bed
already!"

Each day they added
more parts
to the machine.

And each day
it grew bigger
and bigger.

Until one day...
it was finished!

"It's a surprise,
Mama.
Just for you."
"A Time Machine."

"Go inside!
Go ahead!"
"It's what you've
always wanted."

Sally
started the machine.
It began to
rattle
and shake.

"Something's wrong!"
said Sally's father.

"Some present!"
said Sally's mother.

"Are you
all right,
Mama?"

An hour later
Sally's father
came out of the machine.

"I fixed it!
The wires
on the transporter
were crossed."

"HUGO!"

"PAPA!"

"What's the matter
with you two?"
he asked.
And he went
upstairs
for something
to eat.

"How did that
chicken
get into the
house?"

But he did
see one
in the mirror...
and it was
looking out
at him!
He jumped twice.
The chicken
did the same.

Sally's father
looked
all around.
He didn't see
any chicken.

"It's me!
I'm
the chicken!"

Sally's father
ran back inside
the machine.
But nothing changed.

"What should I do…?"
"Wait till
tomorrow, dear.
Maybe things
will be different."

Lunch
was on the table.

"Eggs?
I'm not eating any *eggs!*"
he said,
pushing them away.
"But dear,
they were always
your favorite,"
said his wife.

"Well,
I don't like them
any more.
I'd rather have
some kernels of corn.
And not on a plate.
Scatter them on the floor."

After lunch,
Sally's father
sat in his
favorite chair.
He tried to read,
but he couldn't
concentrate.
He turned on the TV,
but turned it
right off.

"Hugo!
You're dropping feathers
all over the place.
The house
is getting to look
like a barn."

So Sally's father
went out on the porch
to sit.
He watched Sally
coming up the walk
with all her friends.
But when they
reached the gate
Sally
made them wait
outside.

"That's not nice, Sally.
Invite your friends in,"
her father said.
"I will, Papa...."

"Only five cents
to see the biggest chicken
in the world ...."
One by one
the children
filed past.

"Are you
still Sally's
father?"

"Can you
lay an egg
for us?"

"Do an
Easter egg."

By evening
everyone in town
knew about it.

Curious neighbors
kept ringing
the doorbell.
Sally's father
locked himself
in his bedroom.

The next day was no different.

"Hugo,"
said his wife,
"Sally and I
can't live like this
any more.
One of us
has to go...."

The barn wasn't
too uncomfortable
for Sally's father.
But it was
noisier
than the house.

"Still,
it's for the best,"
he said.

At suppertime
Sally scattered
chicken feed.
"Papa,
if you're gonna be
a chicken forever,
can I have your
video recorder
and your gold watch
and the pencil that writes
in four colors and ...?"

Sally's father
was becoming
very depressed.
One minute
he would stare
straight ahead.

The next minute
he would
jump up
and run around the barn.
"Oh, Sally,"
said her mother,
"Papa's getting worse.
I don't know
what to do!"

Cluck!

Cluck!

Cluck!

Cluck!

Cluck!

But Sally did.
She took the
chicken feed
and made a path
from the barn
to the basement
of their house.

When her father
was inside the machine
Sally pulled the chain
to start it.
"Maybe this time
Papa will come out like
Papa."

A few minutes later
the door opened
slowly.
Sally's father
was no longer
a chicken.

"Look!
No feathers!"

Sally
made her father
go back
inside the machine.
When he came out,
it was worse.

Tweet!

Moo!

Woof!

Squeak!

And it kept getting
worse!
It was awful!

And then it happened.
A loud sputter!
A crash!
The invention
was falling
apart.
It collapsed
in a heap!
And in the
middle
of it all
stood Sally's father.

"Papa!
Papa!"

"I found out
what we did wrong,
Sally."

"Don't talk now,
Papa."

"Drink some water,
Hugo."

Sally
and her father
didn't waste
any time
rebuilding the machine.

"Mama says
after this
not to make her
any more presents."

A few days later
it was finished.

They first
tried it out
with an apple...
to make sure
it worked.

"Hooray!"

Then Sally's father
went to get
his wife.

"Go ahead, m'dear.
Go inside."

"I'm going."

Grrr . . .

Sally's mother
made herself comfortable.
Sally
pressed the button.
The machine
began to shake...

...and shake.
When it stopped
shaking,
Sally's mother
was gone!

Ten minutes later
Sally
and her father
received a
long-distance telephone call.
"Hello, Hugo!
I thought you said
I was going
to Florida...."